HENRY

JAMES

PERCY

MEET ALL THESE FRIENDS IN BUZZ BOOKS:

Thomas the Tank Engine
The Animals of Farthing Wood
Biker Mice From Mars
James Bond Junior
Fireman Sam
Joshua Jones
Rupert
Babar

First published 1992 by Buzz Books
an imprint of Reed Children's Books
Michelin House, 81 Fulham Road, London SW3 6RB
and Auckland, Melbourne, Singapore and Toronto

Reprinted 1993 (Twice)

ISBN 185591 210 4

Printed and bound in Italy by Olivotto

BOCO THE DISEASEL

buzz books

Bill and Ben are twin tank engines who live
at the port near Edward's station.

Each has four wheels, a tiny chimney
and dome, and a small squat cab.

The twins are kept busy pulling trucks for engines on the main line, and for ships in the harbour.

Their trucks are filled with china clay dug from the nearby hills. China clay is important. It is needed for pottery, paper, paint and many other things.

One morning, they arranged some trucks and went away for more. They returned to find them all gone.

The twins were most surprised.

Their drivers examined a patch of oil. "That's a diesel," they said, wiping the rails clean.

"It's a what'll?" asked Bill.

"A *diseasel*, I think," replied Ben. "There's a notice about them in our shed."

"I remember, *'coughs and sneezles spread diseasels'*," said Bill.

"Who had a cough in his smoke box yesterday?" said Ben.

"Fireman cleared it, didn't he?" said Bill.

"Yes, but the dust made him sneezle: so there you are," said Ben, huffily. "It's *your* fault the diseasel came."

"It isn't!"

"It is!"

"Stop arguing, you two," said their drivers. "Come on! Let's go and rescue our trucks."

Bill and Ben were horrified. "But the diseasel will magic us away like the trucks!" they said.

Their drivers laughed. "He won't magic us," they said. "We'll more likely magic him! Listen – he doesn't know you're twins, so we'll take away your names and numbers and then this is what we'll do . . ."

Bill and Ben chuckled with delight. "Come on! Let's go!" they said eagerly.

Puffing hard, the twins set off on their journey to find the diesel. They were looking forward to playing tricks on him.

Creeping into the yard, they found the diesel on a siding with the missing trucks.

Ben hid behind, but Bill went boldly alongside.

The diesel looked up. "Do you mind?"
he asked.

"Yes," said Bill. "I do. I want my trucks,
please."

"These are mine," said the diesel.
"Go away."

Bill pretended to be frightened. "You're a big bully," he whimpered. "You'll be sorry." He ran back and hid behind the trucks on the other side.

Ben now came forward. "Truck stealer!"
he hissed.

Then he ran away too and Bill took his
place.

This went on and on till the diesel's eyes nearly popped out.

"Stop!" he begged. "You're making me giddy."

The two engines gazed at him. "Are there two of you?" he asked, in a daze.

"Yes, we're twins," chimed Bill and Ben.

"I might have known it," groaned the diesel.

Just then Edward bustled up. "Bill and Ben, why are you playing here?" he said, crossly.

"We're *not* playing," protested Bill.

"We're rescuing our trucks," squeaked Ben.

"What do you mean?" asked Edward.

"Even *you* don't take our trucks without asking, but this diseasel did!" they both squeaked indignantly.

25

"There's no cause to be rude," said
Edward. "This engine is a Metropolitan
Vickers Diesel-Electric, Type 2."

The twins were abashed. "We're sorry Mr
– er . . ." they stammered.

"Never mind," the diesel smiled. "Call me Boco. I'm sorry I didn't understand about the trucks."

"That's all right, then," said Edward. "Now off you go, Bill and Ben. Fetch Boco's trucks, then you can take this lot."

The twins scampered away. Edward smiled. "There's no real harm in them," he said to Boco, "but they're maddening at times."

Boco chuckled. "Maddening," he said, "is the word."

THOMAS

EDWARD

GORDON